MW00965032

America's First Peoples

The Sioux

Nomadic Buffalo Hunters

by Rachel A. Koestler-Grack

Consultant:
Raymond J. DeMallie
Professor of Anthropology
Indiana University

Blue Earth Books

an imprint of Capstone Press
Mankato, Minnesota

Blue Earth Books are published by Capstone Press
151 Good Counsel Drive, P.O. Box 669, Mankato, Minnesota 56002
http://www.capstone-press.com

Library of Congress Cataloging-in-Publication Data
Koestler-Grack, Rachel A., 1973–
    The Sioux: nomadic buffalo hunters / by Rachel A. Koestler-Grack.
    p. cm. — (America's first peoples)
    Summary: Discusses the Sioux Indians, focusing on their tradition of hunting bison. Includes a recipe for pemmican and instructions for
making a paper buffalo robe.
    Includes bibliographical references and index.
    ISBN 0-7368-1540-6 (hardcover)
    1. Dakota Indians—Juvenile literature. 2. Dakota Indians—Hunting—Juvenile literature. 3. American bison—Juvenile literature.
[1. Dakota Indians. 2. Teton Indians. 3. Indians of North America—Great Plains. 4. American bison.] I. Title. II. Series.
E99.D1 K64 2003
978.004'9752—dc21

2002012540

Editorial credits
Editor: Megan Schoeneberger
Series designer: Kia Adams
Photo researcher: Jo Miller
Product planning editor: Karen Risch

Cover images: *Buffalo Chase, Bulls Making Battle with Men and
Horses,* by George Catlin, by Stock Montage, Inc.; arrows by
Marilyn "Angel" Wynn

Photo credits
AP/Wide World Photos/Susan Walsh, 28–29
Art Resource/Smithsonian American Art Museum, Washington,
    D.C., 18
Aurora/Jeff Jacobson, 29 (right)
Capstone Press/Gary Sundermeyer, 3 (both), 19, 27 (both)
Corbis/Bettmann, 11 (right); Geoffrey Clements, 12–13; Darrell
    Gulin, 24–25
Getty Images/Hulton Archive, 4–5
Marilyn "Angel" Wynn, 8 (right), 16, 20–21, 25 (top right)
Minnesota Historical Society, 17; James Methven, 26
Nebraska State Historical Society Photograph Collections, 22
North Wind Picture Archives, 6, 7, 14, 15, 25 (bottom right)
PhotoDisc, Inc., 8 (top left, bottom left), 9
Rockwell Museum of Western Art, Corning, New York, 10–11
Sid Richardson Collection of Western Art, 21 (right)
TimePix/Keri Pickett, 23

1 2 3 4 5 6 08 07 06 05 04 03

Contents

On page 15, practice your running speed with a Sioux relay race.

Make pemmican with peanut butter on page 19.

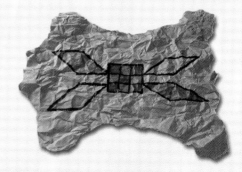

Learn how to decorate a paper buffalo robe on page 27.

Chapter One

Where the Buffalo Roamed

Many years ago, herds of wild buffalo covered the Great Plains. They grazed on grasslands stretching from the Mississippi River in present-day Minnesota to what is now northeastern Wyoming. Searching for fresh grass, about 75 million buffalo moved freely across the open land. At times, the ground shook as buffalo ran across the plains.

Early Sioux Indians left their homes near the headwaters of the Mississippi River. They traveled south to the Minnesota River. From there, buffalo spread out across the plains as far as the Sioux could see. As the seasons changed, the buffalo moved on in search of food. The Sioux followed. In time, Sioux land stretched as far as the buffalo roamed.

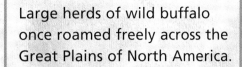

Large herds of wild buffalo once roamed freely across the Great Plains of North America.

The Sioux Name

In the 1600s, French traders came to the Mississippi River. They first met the Ojibwa. These native peoples called their neighbors by a word that meant "enemies." The French shortened the long Ojibwa word to "Sioux."

Today, many Sioux like to use their tribal names. Three tribes make up the Sioux Nation. The Teton Sioux live west of the Missouri River. They call themselves Lakota. The Yankton and Santee Sioux live east of the Missouri River. They call themselves Dakota.

Chapter Two

Following the Herd

In winter, huge snow drifts covered the Great Plains. To eat the grass under the snow, buffalo pushed the snow with their large heads. When the snow melted, they ate the grass until it was gone. They then traveled to a new feeding ground. Herds kept moving to wherever the grass grew tall and thick.

The Sioux often moved their camps to follow the buffalo. When it was time to move, Sioux women took down the tents they called tepees. The cone-shaped homes were made of

As the seasons passed, the Sioux moved their camps to follow the buffalo herds.

several buffalo skins. The skins were sewn together and stretched over tall poles.

At first, women folded the skins and carried them on their backs. In later years, they used horses or dogs to carry the load. The women quickly set up the tepees at the new camp.

The Sioux lived in tepees made of buffalo skins and wooden poles. They could easily move their tepees to a new camp.

Sioux Months

The Sioux did not use calendars. They kept track of months by watching the moon. Each month, the moon grew full, then smaller until it disappeared. It then grew full again. The Sioux called the time from one full moon to another a "moon." Each moon was about one month long. They named the moons by what was happening around them.

January	Moon of the Frost in the Tepee
February	Moon of the Dark Red Calf
March	Moon of Snow Blindness
April	Moon of Green Grass Growing
May	Moon of Shedding Ponies
June	Moon of Making Fat
July	Moon of Red Cherries
August	Moon of Black Cherries
September	Moon when Calves Grow Hair
October	Moon of the Changing Season
November	Moon of Falling Leaves
December	Moon of Popping Trees

Chapter Three

Sioux Hunting Scouts

After the new camp was set up, some Sioux men had the job of searching for the buffalo herd. They were the tribe's hunting scouts. When the scouts found the herd, they returned to camp.

When the scouts returned, they met with tribal leaders. They took turns smoking a special pipe. After the scouts met with the tribal leaders, the hunters began to get ready. They sharpened their arrowheads and practiced shooting on horseback. Young boys watched the hunters to learn how to kill the buffalo.

The Sioux asked the spirits to help them hunt buffalo.

Crazy Horse

Crazy Horse was a Sioux who lived in the mid-1800s. He was a good horseman, hunter, and fighter. Crazy Horse fought to keep white settlers from taking Sioux land. He wanted his people to keep their traditional way of life.

Crazy Horse helped lead the Sioux against the U.S. Army in the Battle of the Little Bighorn. The Sioux won this battle.

Today, people honor Crazy Horse's memory. His image is being carved into a mountain in the Black Hills of South Dakota.

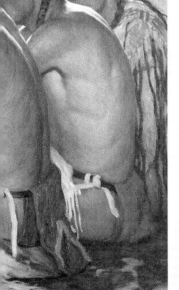

Chapter Four

A Buffalo Hunt

Buffalo were not easy to kill. Hunters rode on horseback to reach the grazing herd. Wind carried the smell of the hunters to the buffalo. With this warning, the animals went running across the prairie. When frightened, the buffalo ran fast. Hunters needed horses to keep up with running herds.

Hunters on horseback circled around a herd. Yelling loudly, they rushed at the buffalo. The hunters stayed close, keeping their bows and arrows ready. As the buffalo ran, the hunters shot arrows. They aimed for the buffalo's stomach or heart. They needed to be close to the buffalo. The arrows had to go deep into the buffalo's thick skin.

Horses helped the hunters keep up with the fast-running buffalo.

13

It was a great honor to be a Sioux hunter. Hunters used special markings on their arrows. They could tell who killed a buffalo. Each hunter kept track of the number of buffalo he killed.

Even before they had horses, hunters set up a buffalo jump. They chased after the buffalo until the animals ran over a cliff. The buffalo would fall to the bottom. Hunters could easily kill the hurt buffalo.

Sioux sometimes chased buffalo over the edge of a cliff.

Sioux Relay Race

Before they had horses, Sioux hunters had to be able to run very fast. They often challenged each other to foot races to test their speed. You and your friends can practice running quickly by playing this game.

What You Need
6 cones or other markers
20 players

What You Do

1. Make a starting line by placing two cones 10 steps apart. Walk 10 steps out from the first two cones and place two more cones. Then walk 20 steps and place the last two cones.

2. Divide players into four teams. Two teams line up for the race behind the starting line cones.

3. The other two teams stand between the second and third row of cones. They will act as trees, streams, and mountains. Trees stand with arms out like branches and twist. Streams wave up and down by bending their knees and reaching for the sky. Mountains do jumping jacks in place.

4. Each runner runs around the trees, streams and mountains. The next runner begins when the runner in front reaches the last cone.

5. The first team to have all its runners make it around the trees, streams, and mountains wins the race.

6. Runners switch places with the trees, streams, and mountains group, and the race begins again.

Chapter Five

After the Kill

After the hunt, men and women cut the skins.
They rolled the skin back from the buffalo
meat. They carefully cut the meat from the
bones. The Sioux hung fresh buffalo skins over
the back of their horses. They then laid large
pieces of cut meat on top of the buffalo skins.
Everyone headed back to camp.

In camp, the women sliced the meat into
thin, flat strips. They hung the strips on wooden
drying racks. Women kept careful watch over
the racks while the meat dried. Birds and dogs
often tried to eat the meat. The women swung
clubs to scare away animals and birds.

*The Sioux cut the buffalo skin away
from the meat in large sheets.*

Back at the camp, strips of meat were hung on wooden racks to dry.

All over the Sioux camp, cooking fires burned. People roasted meat from the buffalo's hump and ribs. Everyone in the village joined in a huge feast with dancing and singing.

The village celebrated a successful buffalo hunt. The hunt was important for the Sioux's survival.

Peanut Butter Pemmican

Sioux women mixed buffalo meat and dried fruit to make pemmican. This mixture kept fresh through the long winter. Sioux Indians mixed the meat and fruit with buffalo fat. This modern recipe uses peanut butter. It holds the ingredients together like buffalo fat did.

What You Need

Ingredients

1 cup (240 mL) beef jerky

2 cups (480 mL) dried apples

1 cup (240 mL) dried cherries

1 cup (240 mL) sunflower seeds

1 tablespoon (15 mL) honey

⅓ cup (80 mL) peanut butter

Equipment

dry-ingredient measuring cups

food processor

large bowl

wooden spoon

microwavable bowl

measuring spoons

drinking glass

8-inch (20-centimeter) square baking pan

knife

What You Do

1. Have an adult grind the jerky and dried fruit in a food processor.
2. Pour the jerky and fruit mixture into a large bowl.
3. Mix in the sunflower seeds.
4. In the microwavable bowl, heat honey and peanut butter in a microwave for 1 minute. Stir mixture until it is smooth.
5. Add the peanut butter mixture to the bowl with the jerky, fruit, and nuts. Mix well.
6. Press the mixture into baking pan using the flat bottom of a drinking glass.
7. Chill pan in refrigerator for several hours until firm.
8. Use a knife to cut the pemmican into squares.

Makes 64 pieces

Chapter Six

Scraping the Skins

As the meat dried, women worked on the buffalo skins. They stretched the skins very tightly. The edges were held in the ground with sharp wooden stakes.

Women made the buffalo skins soft. First, they removed the hair and scraped the skins. They rubbed the skins with buffalo fat and brains. This oily mixture kept the skins from cracking.

Finally, women washed the skins. They rubbed them back and forth. The skins had to be soft enough to use for clothing or tepees.

To dry the buffalo skins, women stretched them across the ground and held them in place with wooden stakes.

Counting Coup

Sioux tried to be generous, wise, strong, and brave. Warriors showed bravery by counting coup. During battle, a warrior moved closer and closer to his enemy. Finally, he could reach out and touch the other person. To touch an enemy was called counting coup.

Small boys played a game called counting coup. They tried to steal a small bit of meat from the drying racks. Usually, the women chased the boys away. Other times, the women played along and pretended not to see the boys. As a woman turned away, she pushed a small piece of meat off the rack with a stick.

Sometimes, the Sioux painted decorations on buffalo skin. They set the decorated skin on a hill above the hunting ground. This skin was a gift of thanks to the Sioux Creator, Wakantanka.

Sioux sometimes painted pictures onto buffalo skins. The pictures told a story or recorded an event.

The White Buffalo Woman Legend

The rarest of all buffalo is the white buffalo. The Sioux believe a white calf is a sign of peace and balance. This story tells why the Sioux believe the white buffalo is special.

One day, two Sioux hunters climbed onto a high hill. Their eyes searched across the prairie and into the faraway hills. They looked for a

sign of the buffalo herd. After some time, they saw a large, white form. At first, the form looked like a white buffalo. As it came closer, they saw it was a beautiful woman.

The first hunter reached out to touch the woman. Suddenly, a large cloud of black smoke came down from the sky. It covered the man, and he was gone. The second hunter fell to his knees.

"Do not be afraid of me," the woman said to him. She told the man to hurry to his camp. She wanted him to build a large lodge where they could meet with her.

Several days later, the villagers heard singing at the edge of camp. Slowly, the beautiful woman walked toward the camp. She wore a white buffalo-skin dress.

The woman gave the villagers a pipe with 12 eagle feathers. The pipe had the power to send the people's prayers to Wakantanka. She began singing again. The woman then turned into a white buffalo and ran away.

Chapter Seven

From Horn to Tail

The Sioux used every part of the buffalo. They found a use for everything, from the horns to the hairs of the tail. They made tools and cooking utensils out of the buffalo horns and bones. A hollowed-out horn made a large soup spoon. Sharp buffalo bones made good sewing needles. They used the tail to brush away biting flies.

The Sioux used buffalo organs such as the bladder to hold water. They made buffalo skins into blankets and clothing. Women sewed pieces of buffalo skin into pillows and stuffed them with buffalo hair.

Every part of the buffalo was useful to the Sioux.

This spoon was made from a buffalo's horn.

The Sioux used a buffalo shoulder blade to make this gardening tool.

25

Inside the Tepee

The tepee was a comfortable home for a Sioux family. Buffalo-skin curtains hung around the inside of the tepee. The Sioux painted stories onto the skins. Beds, covered with buffalo robes, lined the sides of the tepee.

During winter, the family kept a fire burning in the center of the tepee. Smoke from the fire drifted up into the top. In time, the buffalo skin near the top hardened and became nearly waterproof. The family often saved this part of the tepee to make shoes called moccasins.

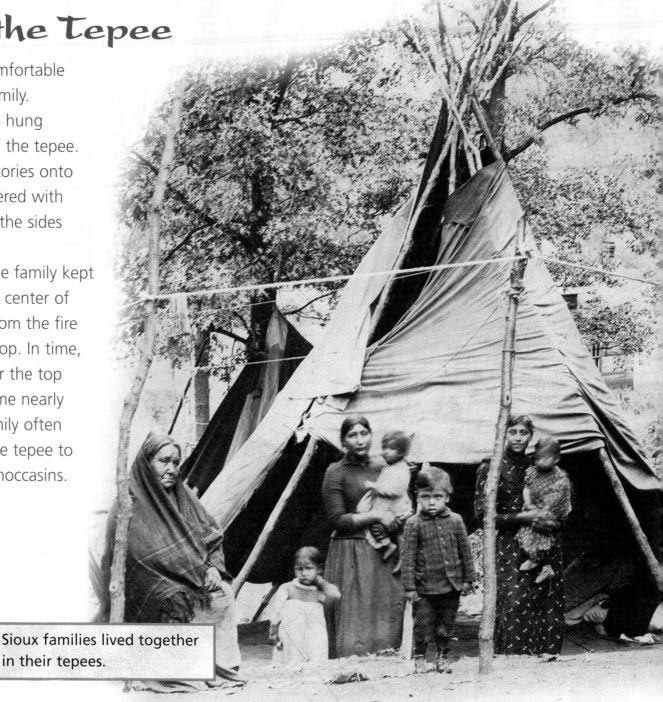

Sioux families lived together in their tepees.

Decorate a Buffalo Robe

Sioux Indians used many designs to decorate their clothing. Women made some designs by sewing beads onto moccasins. Men made other designs by painting on buffalo skin robes. You can make a paper buffalo robe and color a design on it.

What You Need

large paper grocery bag
water
colored markers

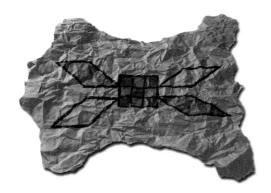

What You Do

1. Tear the bag along the seam and lay it flat.
2. Tear the paper into a buffalo skin shape.
3. Crumple the buffalo skin shape into a ball.
4. Run water over the crumpled paper for a few seconds. The paper should be wet but not soaking.
5. Squeeze out any extra water from the paper.
6. Carefully open the wet paper and lay it outdoors in the sun until it dries.
7. Use colored markers to draw and color a design on the dried buffalo skin. Use the symbols as shown in the photos or make up your own.

Chapter Eight

The Sioux Today

Today, the Sioux do not live in tepees or go on buffalo hunts as they did in the 1800s. The U.S. government has set aside land for the Sioux. These areas are called reservations. The Pine Ridge Reservation in South Dakota is the second largest Indian reservation in the United States.

The buffalo are mostly gone from the Great Plains. But the Sioux people remain. In fact, they are one of the largest American Indian groups in the United States. They remember the buffalo as the source of their strength.

The Sioux teach their children about their traditional way of life.

The Sioux remember when their land was covered by herds of buffalo.

Words to Know

bladder (BLAD-ur)—the body part that stores liquid waste before it leaves the body

counting coup (KOUNT-ing KU)—touching an enemy; Sioux warriors considered this act proof of bravery.

headwaters (HED-waw-turz)—the beginning or source of a river or stream

moccasin (MOK-uh-suhn)—a soft shoe made of animal skin

nomadic (noh-MA-dik)—having a way of life that involves traveling from place to place

Ojibwa (oh-JIB-wah)—an American Indian tribe living in the Great Lakes region of the United States; the Ojibwa were neighbors of the Sioux.

pemmican (PEH-mi-kuhn)—a dried mixture of buffalo meat, fat, and fruit

reservation (rez-ur-VAY-shuhn)—land owned and controlled by American Indians

scout (SKOUT)—someone sent to find and bring back information

traditional (truh-DISH-uhn-uhl)—having to do with the ways of the past

Wakantanka (wah-KAHN-tahn-kuh)—the name the Sioux call their Creator

To Learn More

Isaacs, Sally Senzell. *Life in a Sioux Village.* Picture the Past. Chicago: Heinemann Library, 2002.

Lund, Bill. *The Sioux Indians.* Native Peoples. Mankato, Minn.: Bridgestone Books, 1998.

Rose, LaVera. *Grandchildren of the Lakota.* World's Children. Minneapolis: Carolrhoda Books, 1999.

Todd, Anne M. *Crazy Horse, 1842–1877.* American Indian Biographies. Mankato, Minn.: Blue Earth Books, 2003.

Places to Write and Visit

Akta Lakota Museum

St. Joseph's Indian School

North Main Street

P.O. Box 89

Chamberlain, SD 57325

Crazy Horse Memorial

Avenue of the Chiefs

Crazy Horse, SD 57730-9506

Minnesota Historical Society

345 West Kellogg Boulevard

St. Paul, MN 55102-1906

Museum of the South Dakota State Historical Society

Cultural Heritage Center

900 Governors Drive

Pierre, SD 57501-2217

Internet Sites

Track down many sites about the Sioux.
Visit the FACT HOUND at *http://www.facthound.com*

IT IS EASY! IT IS FUN!

1) Go to *http://www.facthound.com*
2) Type in: 0736815406
3) Click on "FETCH IT" and FACT HOUND will find several links hand-picked by our editors.

Relax and let our pal FACT HOUND do the research for you!

Index